The Creatures Of Chichester

The one about the mystery blaze.

Christopher Joyce

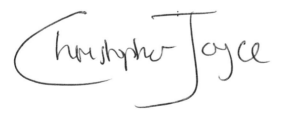

DEDICATION
To Bernard

With thanks to Eric, and Gerry for their editing skills and Joe Elgie for his amazing illustrations.

Published by
Chichester Publishing
Copyright © 2014 Christopher Joyce.

ISBN-13: 978 0 9929899 2 7
ISBN-10: 0992989922

CONTENTS

1 CLOWN SOUP

They came in the middle of the night with two large axes that broke through the kitchen door. All of the alarms started wailing so loudly that everyone was awake in a few seconds.

Shandy mostly slept through the day and liked to exercise late at night with her twin sister, Mash. They would often have a late night snack of salad, and perhaps a drink of water, before getting on to their exercise wheels for a thirty-minute workout.

Although they were twins, they

weren't identical. Shandy was older by two minutes and always reminded Mash of that fact. She was in good shape for a hamster. Her golden fur shone in the moonlight as she ran on her wheel. Mash was a little more round and the colour of fluffy potato, which was how she got her name. It so happens that Mash was also a little less excited than Shandy by almost everything that went on around them. Shandy was bubbly by nature. Mash was not. All in all, they were well named by their owner, a young Twoleg called Gilbert.

He had brought them home from school about a year ago when they were very young. His stepfather had not been very keen on the idea of having rodents in the pub, but his mother had said that as long as he promised to look after them and never let them out into the restaurant, it would be okay.

'Did you hear that?' asked Shandy. She stopped running so suddenly in her wheel that it went around one full turn with her hanging on for dear life.

'Yes, it's probably nothing,' replied Mash, who was just about to enjoy a nice crunchy carrot that she'd found hidden under a slightly limp bit of lettuce. Then the alarms stopped abruptly, and they could hear muffled shouting as the lights were switched on all over the pub. The Twolegs started running around in all directions.

Down in the kitchen, the thieves had been startled by

the alarms and were frozen to the spot. They were dressed completely in black and wore clown masks that covered their faces. They dropped their axes and ran towards the broken door as fast as their legs could carry them.

But there was not room for both of them to squeeze past the rack of plates that were piled up high. With one almighty crash, the rack tipped over and the plates shattered on the stone floor. One of the Twolegs stretched out his hand to balance himself and accidentally pulled over a vat of chicken soup that was being prepared for the next day.

The soup poured down on top of him. He fell to the floor

right in the path of the second clown, whose mask had slipped over her eyes in the panic to get out of the kitchen. She tripped over her partner, bathed in soup, and slammed into a trolley full of knives and forks. The trolley sped across the kitchen and smashed into a wall.

With a deafening crash, it bounced back towards the soup-covered clowns and showered them with knives and forks. They looked a bit like a circus act that had gone horribly wrong, with cutlery sticking out of the wall behind them.

They just managed to get to their feet and out through the gaping hole in the door when Gilbert's stepfather rushed into the kitchen, carrying a baseball bat. Everything around him was chaos, but the burglars were gone. All that was left for the police to examine, when they arrived thirty minutes later, were just two clown masks covered in chicken soup.

Gilbert had woken suddenly. His first thought was to protect his hamsters. He was checking that Shandy and Mash were okay when his mother shouted to him to stay upstairs and lock the door.

'Why does this keep on happening?' he asked the hamsters, not really expecting a reply.

This was the third time in two months that someone had broken into the pub. Each time it was more serious. The first time, they'd just smashed a few eggs; the second time, they stole the microwave. That's when his stepfather had put in the alarm system, but they still had no idea why they were being targeted. All Gilbert knew was that things were not going well. His mother and stepfather often stayed up late going over the books, trying not to show how worried they really were.

Most of the Twolegs in Chichester were looking forward to Christmas, which was just a few weeks away. Although everyone was keeping an eye on how much they spent, Trents in South Street had been doing quite well. It had always been a popular pub with lovely pictures of the surrounding hills and beaches on its cream-coloured walls and a sunny patio where the Twolegs would gather in the summer months to meet friends for lunch.

Everyone liked the friendly staff, and the new Christmas menu was proving to be a great hit too.

The music nights were beginning to attract more people to the pub. Gilbert used to sneak down with the hamsters in his pocket to listen to the latest band, even though he knew he'd be in big trouble if his mum caught him. Shandy loved to do a funny little hamster dance to all the latest hits. Mash would just shake her head as her sister wobbled back and forth on her short, stubby legs.

On one of these late night visits, the hamsters had climbed just high enough out of Gilbert's pocket to watch the Twolegs chatting and flirting with each other. Everyone was having a good time, except a couple of Twolegs tucked away at a table by the bar. They were glaring at all the other drinkers, as if they were evil goblins about to steal their Christmas presents. The couple in the corner were dressed all in black and hid their faces as they sipped their drinks.

Shandy couldn't quite hear what they were saying to each other, but after a few words, they grabbed their bags from under the table and wove their way through the dancing throng towards the door. A pretty blonde Twoleg bumped into one of them knocking his bag off his shoulder. Shandy gasped as she saw two scary clown masks fall out onto the floor. They looked just like the ones left behind after the break-in.

'It's time for us to do a bit of investigation,' she whispered to Mash, who watched the Twolegs push aside the blonde lady and storm out of the pub.

2 THE CATCHA-CLOWN-ASAURUS

The police had been at the pub all morning. It had taken several hours to clear up the mess left by the clown-masked robbers. The kitchen was almost back to normal. The broken door had been replaced, and customers were beginning to arrive for lunch, but all was not well.

Gilbert's mum and stepfather were quarrelling again. It was the same argument they'd been having for several weeks now. They had shut the living room door so Gilbert couldn't hear them, but Shandy and Mash were still awake after the excitement of the previous night. They crawled to the front of their cage to listen more carefully.

It seemed that another buyer was interested in taking over the pub, but Gilbert's mum was not keen to move again. She said that it wasn't fair to Gilbert, who was settling in nicely to his new school, and that this would be the third time they'd moved in as many years. Her husband tried to keep calm. He explained that with all the break-ins and costs of repairing the damage, they simply couldn't afford to keep going. He placed his hand gently on his wife's shoulder and suggested that this buyer might be different. This time it would all work out.

At that point, Gilbert came into the room with a big smile on his face. He'd drawn a picture of a dinosaur chasing off the bad men with the clown masks and gave it to his mum. She smiled for the first time that day and ruffled his hair as she admired the picture of the huge green creature. It had bulging eyes and dozens of teeth snapping at the legs of the fleeing clowns.

Gilbert told them it was a Catcha-clown-asaurus and that it would save them from any further break-ins. They all laughed, and Gilbert said he was going to feed his hamsters. He picked up the cage and headed to the kitchen.

'I wouldn't want to meet one of those Catcha-clown-asauruses,' said Mash as she tucked into a nice bowl of apple and banana.

'They wouldn't bother you unless they were Catcha-hamster-asauruses,' said Shandy, who was feeling a little bit happier now that the mood in the pub had improved. She was still determined to help find the masked Twolegs that had caused all the problems. 'We ought to get the help of those spiders from North Street,' she said. 'You know, the ones that helped catch the dog thief in the summer.'

Now, it was a fact that these two spiders had become quite famous amongst the creatures of Chichester. They had, somehow, managed to get the other animals to trust each other and all work together to catch the Twoleg who had stolen a lovely little puppy called Streak from the butcher's shop.

'I hear that they're still on tour,' said Mash, who had finished her fruit and was now eyeing some tasty cucumber. 'One of the mice that had been involved in the rescue told me they'd all be meeting at the Market Cross tonight. He said that they expected a large crowd of creatures to gather there. Even the famous falcon, Crypt, might make an appearance.'

'Well then, we need to go up to the cross and ask them for help,' said Shandy. 'We'll have to do the pip-in-the-lock trick again tonight to get out of the cage.'

Mash shook her head in despair. This sounded like another of Shandy's great adventures. Mash would much rather be curled up on a nice bed of straw, but doubted she would get the chance tonight. Shandy carefully slid a large, hard apple pip into the locking mechanism of their cage. It was just large enough to stop the bar from sliding across, and she hoped that Gilbert would not notice it when he came to say goodnight.

She was excited about a midnight trip to the Market Cross. It was in the centre of the old city and had been there for hundreds of years. It was more like a huge stone crown that sheltered the Twolegs from the rain as they gathered to gossip about the day's events.

Trents was a few hundred metres down South Street, which led directly to the cross.

West Street led from the cross to the magnificent cathedral home of Pulpit and Crypt, the famous peregrine falcons that the Twolegs had been photographing all summer long. In fact, a Twoleg had even climbed up to the turrets of the cathedral and placed a video camera in the nest. Pulpit had told everyone that she was absolutely outraged by the intrusion into her private life. But her husband, Crypt, told his close friends that his wife secretly cleaned the lens each morning to make sure that her adoring public got a good view.

The falcon once said that from high above the cathedral, the city looked like a huge wheel with the cross at its centre. The streets were the spokes of the wheel that reached out from the cross to the ancient walls that circled the city like a punctured tyre.

Later that night, Gilbert brought a little fresh water, said goodnight to his hamsters, and pushed the door catch in place. It hit the apple pip and stopped just short of the lock. Shandy and Mash pretended to be asleep, but as soon as he was gone, Shandy quietly pushed at the door of their cage. It didn't budge. Mash moaned quietly to herself and made one huge shove. The door flew open.

'I told you that you ought to eat more,' she said to her sister as she hopped out into the lounge. 'If you had a bit more flesh on your bones, you wouldn't need me to do all the heavy work.'

They soon found themselves downstairs by the old kitchen door. Luckily, the repairs had not been perfect, and there was just enough space for them to crawl out onto the patio. Shandy's whiskers were bristling with excitement at the thought of meeting the spiders of North Street, and although the winter chill made her shiver, even Mash thought it was fun to escape for the night.

Neither of the hamsters noticed the dark shapes of the Twolegs crouching on the roof of the kitchen. They were trying to catch their breath, which was making steaming swirls of silver as the cold air whisked it away. One of the Twolegs placed a clown mask on her head and reached into her bag for a large box of matches, but by then Shandy and Mash were already well on their way to the cross.

3 THE FLAMING INFERNO

The presentation had already begun by the time the hamsters arrived at the old stone cross in the centre of town. The Christmas lights had been turned off, and as usual, the streets were nearly deserted. The few Twolegs who remained were wearing Santa hats and reindeer antlers on their heads. They staggered along, singing the same tunes that had been playing in the shops for the last few months.

None of them wondered why

there seemed to be a large number of birds perched on the turrets of the Market Cross. The birds were listening intently to the tiny spiders hidden in the crown of a long-forgotten king who stared with cold stony eyes down East Street.

All of the creatures gathered there could spink to each other, if they put their minds to it. Just as Twolegs think out loud, creatures can think IN loud and share their thoughts as if they were speaking the same language. It was generally agreed that it was bad form to eat another creature when it was spinking to you. So although the mice gathered under the stone seats looked nervously at the seagulls and pigeons perched high above, they still felt safe-ish.

All in all, there were around thirty creatures tuned into Button. He was the spider that had gathered the creatures together last summer to rescue the puppy, Streak, from his evil captors. He was a very well-presented spider and carried himself with style. All eight of his long, furry legs were always neat and tidy, with never a hair out of place.

His story was coming to an end, and although many of the creatures crouching in the chilly evening breeze had heard the story many times, they still loved to hear it told again. Button had come to the part where he was asking for any questions. He was surprised to see a small hamster come out of the shadows.

'There is something not right

at our pub,' said Shandy. 'We've had several break-ins. There are some very dodgy-looking clowns hanging around late at night, and they don't look like they are there to throw custard pies at each other.'

Button listened to her story, then slid to the ground on a shiny strand of silk in such a graceful manner that some of those gathered sighed gently. He was quickly becoming a big hit among the other creatures, especially the ladybirds, who giggled as they shoved each other aside to get a closer look.

'It sounds like we all need to be on high alert and keep an eye or three out for any funny stuff going on.'

As he said this, he looked into the eight eyes of his little sister, who'd just about had enough of his posing and flirting with the ladybirds. She was seconds away from wrapping him up in a big ball of especially gooey silk when one of the birds let out a cry from the top of the cross.

'It's the pub. It's on fire!'

There is nothing that panics the creatures of Chichester as much as fire. At first everyone was frozen to the spot. Then there was a mass stampede as they headed in all directions. Most were running in the opposite direction of the plumes of black smoke that could be seen drifting up South Street. All except the hamsters, Shandy and Mash, who were running as fast as their little legs could carry them back towards their burning home.

By the time they arrived, a growing crowd of Twolegs had gathered outside the pub. Some of them were holding up mobile phones to film the flames licking at the roof timbers. Others were comforting friends who were choking after inhaling the acrid smoke. Blaring sirens and flashing blue lights lit up the wintery sky, as the Twolegs from the fire station at the top of North Street arrived and began to douse the flames.

The hamsters desperately scanned the crowd, but there was no sign of Gilbert or his parents. Nobody noticed Shandy and Mash dash under the long lengths of shiny yellow tape that had been strung along the street to keep the growing crowd back from the unfolding disaster. The hamsters ignored their instincts to run for safety and instead headed directly towards the flames, feeling the heat scorch their fur as they approached the kitchen.

'Is Gilbert safe? Can you see him?' squeaked Shandy.

'I can't see a thing in all this smoke,' spluttered Mash, hardly able to breathe in the toxic air.

The stairs that they had joyfully scampered down just a short while ago loomed above them, towering cliffs of scorched carpet. Each one now seemed impossible to climb. Mash led the way with her lungs at bursting point and shouted to her sister to stay where she was. But Shandy was not too far behind, determined to discover if Gilbert was all right.

The sound of glass shattering

in the heat and the roar of the flames merged with the screaming and shouting from the Twolegs below. With their eyes streaming, the hamsters headed up to their room above the kitchen. The flames seemed to have started on the roof above, and the lower rooms were not yet alight.

'I'm sure his parents would have taken him out first,' said Shandy, as the curtains in the lounge started to smoulder next to her. Mash had pushed through to the table where their cage was kept.

'It's gone. He came to save us before he saved himself.'

The heat from the flames was now becoming unbearable. As the shouts and screams from the street grew louder, the two hamsters turned towards the

door. The curtains suddenly burst into flames, and the room was full of orange light that cast huge shadows of the hamsters on the lounge wall. For a brief moment they appeared to be massive shadow puppets caught in a bizarre play. Then there was a loud explosion from the gas canisters kept in the kitchen below, and the floor of the lounge collapsed in a burning mass of timbers, fabric, and furniture.

Some of the Twolegs in the street cheered heartlessly as they caught all the action on their mobile phones, but most swayed silently from side to side, holding their loved ones close to them. The ambulances arrived from St Richard's Hospital to care for the injured, as the fire-fighters drenched the pub with gallons of water.

Just behind the ambulances, two figures dressed all in black slid away into the shadows. They dumped their clown masks in a nearby litter bin, as they melted away into the night.

4 TIME TO COME CLEAN

The next day, there was a picture of the fire on the front page of the *Chichester Observer*. Button and Stitchley crawled down from their web to examine it closely. They could see the brave firemen with blackened faces and several frightened Twolegs holding each other tightly, but there was no sign of the hamsters, their owner Gilbert or, indeed, his parents.

The headline in the paper took up much of the front page:

Managers Missing
in Mystery Blaze

It seemed that Gilbert's parents had simply disappeared into the night. Nobody had seen them since the fire engines first arrived. The pub had been searched. A spokesperson had said that there were no bodies inside the building, and they were treating the disappearance as suspicious. The spokesperson went on to say that their son, Gilbert, was recovering from minor burns at St Richard's Hospital and was being cared for by friends of the family.

'This really is a terrible mess,' said Stitchley, crawling closer to the newspaper. 'That hamster was trying to warn us that something was wrong, but she was just too late. I wonder what happened to her and her sister.'

Button was also feeling guilty about spending so much time showing off to some of the other creatures at the cross. If he hadn't been, Shandy would have had more time to explain what was going on.

'It's not your fault,' said Stitchley. 'But I'm sure we can help find the missing Twolegs and those poor hamsters, if they survived the fire. This looks like another job for the Creatures of Chichester.'

'I thought you told me that after nearly being eaten by bats TWICE in our last adventure, we were going to stay put, safe and warm in our little shop in North Street.'

'But you're so brave and clever,' replied Stitchley,

pandering to her brother's new-found fame, 'and the other creatures trust you now. We have to give it a go.'

Button had, indeed, become a bit of a celebrity, and he did get a little bored watching the brides come and go, as they tried on endless versions of wedding gowns, with a gaggle of bridesmaids 'oohing' and 'ahhing' at every new dress.

He much preferred his old home, Marco's, with its sharp, tailored suits and classy leather belts. But Marco's had closed down, and the new bridal shop had taken its place. Stitchley, however, loved it and would spend hours crawling over the wedding magazines, imagining that a strong, handsome spider would one day whisk her away to a silken paradise.

Button looked at the magazines, the endless metres of silk, and the bolts of lace and sighed quietly to himself.

'You're right,' he said. 'Let's get a message to Knuckles and Streak at the butcher's shop. I'll speak to one of the ladybirds to see if they can fly over there and get them to come to the cross for a meeting as soon as possible.'

A family of ladybirds had recently moved into the dry cleaner's a few doors down North Street, and Button had become quite friendly with them.

Most ladybirds try to find a warm dry hiding place to sleep through the winter months, maybe in a warm shed or cosy bedroom. This family had discovered a beautifully warm corner high up above the clothes dryers that hummed away for most of the day. It was like being on a winter vacation on a sunny island far away when everyone else at home was freezing and moaning about the weather. They could not believe their luck.

The head of the family was Blotch. He had six perfectly round spots on his shiny red wing covers and never seemed to rest. When most of the family were happy to just snooze the day away, Blotch was always on the lookout for danger, or maybe a little snack. He had too many children for Button to remember all their names, and he had to admit that it was difficult to be quite sure who was a girl-ladybird and who was a boy-ladybird. In the end he just called them "you bugs" and hoped they weren't offended.

Button met up with Blotch later that night, and the ladybird agreed to fly over to the butcher's the next day to ask the dogs, Knuckles and Streak, to meet them at the cross. Blotch knew that the journey would be difficult in the cold winter air and was secretly a bit frightened about leaving the safety of the warm drycleaner's.

He was still thinking about his perilous journey the next morning when a Twoleg entered the shop. She had a large bag of dry-cleaning over her shoulder and paced back and forth nervously as she waited for the assistant to serve the customers in front of her.

Eventually, it was her turn, and Blotch, suspicious of her odd behaviour, crawled a little closer down the wall to listen to the conversation. She wanted to have some trousers and two jackets cleaned and wondered how soon they would be ready. The assistant told her that it would just take a few days and that she could come and collect the items the following Monday.

Blotch crawled closer still to get a better look and was almost knocked off his six feet by the stench of stale smoke. The assistant also looked a little surprised as she pulled the clothes out of the black plastic bin liner. The customer nervously explained that they had been at a bonfire party ages ago, but had not had a chance to bring in the smoky jackets and trousers because of all the rain. The assistant just nodded and handed over her receipt without another word.

As the Twoleg turned to go, she looked up towards the clock on the wall where Blotch had positioned himself. He thought she was looking right at him, but she was just squinting to see the time clearly. It was then that Blotch recognised her.

On the counter near the till was last week's *Chichester Observer*. The story about the terrible fire had filled four or five pages, and on page two was a picture of Gilbert's mum – not seen since the fire.

That very same face was now staring at the clock on the wall.

She pulled on a dark woolly hat as another customer

entered the shop. She carefully pushed a few loose strands of hair under the rim and shuffled out into a gentle flurry of snow that seemed to curl around her as she disappeared from view. Blotch waited for a few minutes, then crawled back to his family snoozing gently in the warm air. He counted all his children and thanked the Great Animal in the sky that they were all safe and sound. It was going to be a long journey tomorrow.

5 CRISIS AT THE CROSS

Gilbert couldn't remember anything about the fire. His father and his new girlfriend had been with him for three days now, as he recovered in hospital. Gilbert had not seen his father for several years and had a strange mixture of feelings when he awoke and saw his face. He knew that his parents had separated just after he was born. At first he'd seen quite a lot of his dad. But over the years, the visits had become less and less frequent and then they'd stopped altogether.

He'd never met the new girlfriend before. She was a lot younger than his dad and seemed to spend a great deal of time chatting to the young doctors. She was not very interested in him at all. At first, they told him that his mum and stepfather were recovering in another ward, but now, on his third morning after the fire, his father finally told him the truth.

Nobody had seen them since the fire.

Gilbert hid his face in the pillow and sobbed so loudly that the passing nurses stopped in the corridor to see what was happening. His father held his hand and tried to comfort him, but he cried solidly for two hours. He was terrified that he would never see his mum again. The nurses eventually calmed him down and told him that they were definitely not in the building when it had burnt down. They were probably just sorting everything out for when he was better.

But Gilbert knew something was wrong. And what about his pet hamsters? Had anybody seen them?

Button also knew something was very wrong after his conversation with Blotch. The ladybird had told him about the mysterious visitor to the drycleaner's and said that he was quite sure that it was the Twoleg pictured in the newspaper.

'I can't believe that she

wouldn't go to see her son in hospital,' said Stitchley, who had left her web to listen to the two insect-friends chatting.

'I'm sure it was her. She looked just the same.'

'Well, I don't know of any mother that would carry on as normal with their child in hospital. Perhaps she's had a bump on the head and has no memory of the fire or of her son. The poor woman is probably dazed and confused and has no idea about what happened. How awful!'

The weak winter sun was just visible behind the clouds when Blotch set off to get help from Knuckles and Streak at the butcher's. The two dogs were the best of friends and had become even closer after Streak was stolen earlier in the year. Streak was now a slightly wiser puppy and would never go running up to strangers who offered him doggy biscuits. Well, he might sit at their feet and shake his big floppy ears and open his big brown eyes as wide as he could – but he would NEVER run up to them. Stroll slowly in their direction, maybe, but never run.

Knuckles was sort of box shaped with black spots and one droopy ear. Some of the creatures used to call him "The Pirate Pooch" as he had a large black patch over his eye – but not many were brave enough to call him that when they were in the same room. He wasn't a mean dog, but he could stop a Twoleg by just staring at them in a 'your-left-ankle-looks-mighty-tasty' sort of way.

When Blotch arrived at the butcher's, he was quite exhausted. The cold air had sapped his strength as he hadn't eaten a lovely tasty aphid for ages. His landing was not the prettiest he'd ever made. He skidded across the countertop of the butcher's and folded his wings beneath his bright red and black wing case. He stopped for a moment to gather his breath and then spinked to Knuckles, who was standing near the door.

'Are you Knuckles the dog?' asked Blotch.

'No, I'm Puff the Magic Dragon. Who wants to know?'

Blotch explained who he was and why he'd come for help. Knuckles had never really had the time to thank the spiders for their help last summer and did not hesitate to say that he'd do anything he could. He and Streak would be at the cross tomorrow around midnight.

The next evening, as the bells in the cathedral rang out their twelfth and final chime, there was once again a strange collection of creatures gathered under the old stone cross in the centre of town. Button and Stitchley had invited Blotch, Knuckles, and Streak, as well as an old friend from the hospice, Codger.

Codger was a wise (and sometimes just a teeny bit forgetful) mole who all of the creatures knew well. He'd lived in the grounds of St Wilfrid's Hospice for more years than

anyone could remember and would help point them in the right direction. Button updated everyone about the Twoleg in the drycleaner's and the arrival of Gilbert's dad at the hospital.

Codger wiped some dirt away from his tiny little black eyes and spinked clearly to everyone, 'When the smoke clears there may be more than one log on the fire, and a fox loves her cubs even when they spit in her eye!'

The creatures were quite used to Codger's strange sayings. Sometimes they made sense, and sometimes they didn't. Everyone looked a bit confused and waited for an explanation.

'We need to look further afield,' he explained. 'We still need to find the masked clowns. Did anyone see them in town before the fire or know where they are now? I think they hold the answers to this problem.'

They all shook their heads, and nobody spinked until a small voice from the shadows replied, 'They nearly killed us. We thought we'd never survive!'

The group of creatures peered into the gloom to see a weak and badly scorched hamster stagger up the steps of the cross. She had wounds on her back that had still not healed properly, and one eye was closed tightly shut. The fur on the left side of her body was almost all burned away, and her skin looked blistered and sore. She tried to open her mouth to spink but collapsed at the foot of the cross. Streak was the first to reach her and very gently started licking at her wounds.

The others were in shock as she muttered, 'They still have Shandy. We need your hel...'

6 A STING IN THE TALE

Four days had passed since the meeting at the cross. All the creatures that had gathered there had told their friends about the horrific sight of the badly injured hamster. Those friends had told their friends, who told their children, who told their playmates – so the whole city was on full alert.

Button sat in the centre of his web, controlling the flow of information as each sighting of anything suspicious was reported by the city's creatures.

A pigeon had seen two figures in black near the post office late at night. She reported it to a blackbird, who followed them to a red car. She told a tree mouse, who told a vole, who updated Button. Everybody in the city was being watched by an insect, bird, or furry creature of some sort.

It was just a few days until Christmas, so the streets of the city were packed with Twolegs who rushed from one shop to another with bent umbrellas, plastic bags full of presents, and enough food to last until summer. The rain continued to pour down. The creatures sheltered in nooks and crannies as they watched and waited for some news about the missing hamster and Gilbert's parents.

In the Olde Sweet Shoppe,

Caramella had been on high alert ever since the fire. She was not at all amused by being woken up at this time of year. She was, after all, a Queen Bumblebee, and she'd been dreaming of roses and lavender swaying in a gentle breeze when the fire from the pub on the opposite side of South Street had abruptly awoken her.

She was not quite as beautiful as she had been in her youth, but she still had the grace and charm of an Imperial Highness. The long hairs on her body were as soft as silk, and her stripes of black and yellow still dazzled in the sunlight. She had chosen the sweet shop in which to hibernate through the winter because she loved the smell of fudge and toffees and sticky sherbet sweets. They reminded her of the scents and colours of the beautiful flowers near her home in the bishop's gardens near the cathedral.

She hadn't heard the sound of the fire engines or the Twolegs screaming in the street, but the heat and vibrations were enough to wake her from her slumber. Ever since that day, she'd remained wide awake. It was just after lunch when she saw the Twolegs come into her shop.

A man and woman, all dressed in black, were having a big argument as they angrily shovelled pear drops and humbugs into their paper bags. Caramella flew down to the edge of one of the jars to see what was going on. The lady Twoleg said that they couldn't keep their 'guests' hidden for much longer and that they had to get out of town soon. She'd said 'guests' in a strange whisper, almost mouthing the word rather than saying it out loud. Caramella wondered if the 'guests' were really staying with them of their own free will.

She buzzed with excitement as she realised she had to report back to Button about her news. Unfortunately, she buzzed rather loudly, and the male Twoleg was approaching her with a folded up copy of the *Chichester Observer*.

She desperately tried to fly off, but her muscles were still not warm, and she'd only just lifted into the air when the paper came smashing down. The rush of air caused her to tumble backwards in a crazy spin. She just missed the edge of the shop counter and landed dazed on the floor. The Twoleg turned and lifted a huge black boot that came crashing down on top of her, and he slid his foot from side to side.

There was total blackness – but she realised that she was still breathing. She had managed to squeeze into the gap between the Twoleg's heel and the sole of his shoe. As he lifted his foot to look for the squashed bee, she flew out with all the speed she could muster.

Now she WAS warmed up and furious that this ugly Twoleg had tried to squish the life out of her. She headed straight for his large spotty nose and sunk her shiny sting in as far as she could. This was not a grizzly end for Caramella because she was a bumblebee. She neatly withdrew her stinger before getting as far away from the vile creature as she could.

The Twoleg screamed like a little baby as the pain from his nose spread slowly across his face. He went cross-eyed trying to see what had caused such agony. Losing his focus, he did not see Caramella escaping with her life. She landed just a few feet away as he let out yet another blood-curdling scream. He held both hands to his face and was hopping from one leg to another. As this strange dance continued, he fell back towards the counter. He landed in a pile of jelly babies that went spinning into the air like multi-coloured gymnasts. These were quickly followed by a dozen or so sherbet fountains that exploded on the floor

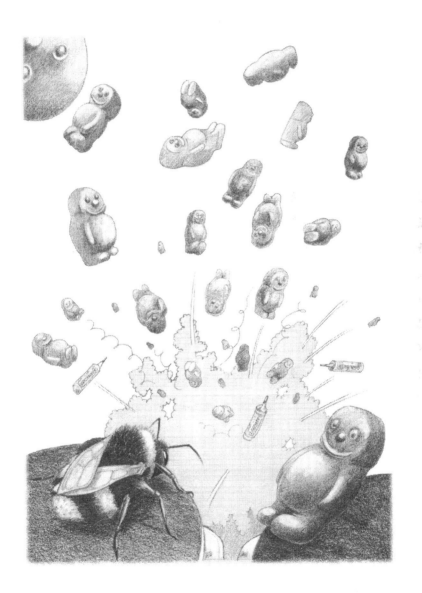

around him, spraying their powdery contents in feathery swirls across his chest.

The shopkeeper had rushed to the front of the shop and was now yelling at the Twolegs, saying that they had to pay for all the damage. But it seemed that they were not too keen to do so and grabbed their bags of sweets and made a dash for the door. As they did, the shopkeeper managed to grab the jacket of the lady fleeing the store and ripped open her pocket.

Some coins, a used tissue, and a piece of paper fell to the floor. Caramella flew down to investigate and realised it was a letter. It began:

Dear Gilbert,

I want you to know that we are both safe and missing you terribly and that we will be with you as soon as we can. Please be a good boy and do exactly what your father asks.

This must all be very strange for you, and I wish I could be there to hold your hand. Your stepdad sends his love and wants you to know that Shandy and Mash are safe and well. He managed to rescue them from the fire.

You are too young to understand why I can't be with you just now, but be very brave, like one of your biggest, toughest, fiercest dinosaurs.

PLEASE KEEP THIS LETTER SECRET AND TELL NOBODY.

We will see you soon.

Love Mummy. Xxxxxx

7 OLD LACE AND BLACKBERRIES

Caramella could not fly fast enough to tell Button the news. The cold air took her breath away as she flew up South Street. It made her realise how wise it was to sleep during the winter months. She was glad of her lovely striped coat, as she beat her wings faster and faster to keep warm. Although the journey only took a few minutes, she arrived at the bridal shop in North Street absolutely exhausted. The two spiders waited for her to catch her breath before spinking to her.

'My goodness,' remarked Stitchley. 'What on earth has happened? I've never seen you in such a panic before. And shouldn't you be asleep at this time of year?'

'My apologies, dear thing,' Caramella replied, regaining some of her grandeur. 'One must think that our arrival is quite, quite shocking for a creature of our position in society. We apologise for this frightfully sudden entrance, but it was rather an emergency.'

The creatures in town were used to Caramella calling herself 'we' in a very posh and royal way. The younger creatures used to look wildly around to see who the others were, but they never found anyone. Their parents would point out that Caramella was really "Her Imperial Highness, Princess Caramella Fudgely-Sherbeton IV, Duchess of Selsey, and Empress of Bognor", which might explain why she thought she was more than one person.

Caramella explained about the letter to the spiders, who listened in stunned silence. After several minutes Button asked, 'So, do you think the Twoleg in the shop was Gilbert's mum?'

'She certainly looked like the one who was in the newspaper after the fire. But we don't know her very well. She rarely comes into my emporium. We wouldn't want to say it was her, but then again, we wouldn't want to say it wasn't.'

'What about the other Twoleg? The one you stung – had you seen him before?'

'No, we don't think we've encountered that Twoleg before, and we certainly have no desire to meet him ever again.'

'Well, the good news is that the letter said that Shandy and Mash are safe,' spinked Stitchley.

Button replied, 'At least they were when the letter was written, but that must have been days ago since we all saw how badly injured Mash was. I wouldn't describe her as "safe and well".' He climbed into the centre of his web and slowly closed his eyes to think.

Gilbert also had his eyes closed tight. He was out of hospital now and staying at his dad's flat, in the centre of town. He was pretending to be asleep. He heard his father say that he was very worried about Gilbert's injuries and that he must be missing his mum.

The new girlfriend didn't seem to care. She applied yet another coat of thick red lipstick to her puffy lips. Gilbert already thought they looked like someone had filled them full of air with a bicycle pump. Now they looked like two red bananas stretched over her face. Not that you could see much of her face. Thick layers of makeup were smudged all over her skin. It reminded Gilbert of the ripples in the sand at the beach in West Wittering. He closed his eyes even tighter and tried to slow his breathing so they'd think he was still asleep.

One of Shandy's eyes was also tightly shut, as the bruising was just healing from the injuries she suffered in the fire. She'd been smashed across the head by a piece of timber falling from the roof. The rest was just a blur of flames, smoke, and shouting. She could vaguely remember being picked up by a Twoleg, who threw her in a plastic carrier bag with Mash. But that was days ago, and since then she'd been nursed by her twin sister, who licked her wounds and made sure she drank fresh water.

She wasn't quite sure where she had been taken. Now she was in some sort of cardboard box that was hidden behind a pile of other boxes. Someone had drilled a few air holes in the side. Through one of the air holes she could see discarded pizza boxes and empty cans of beer. She could just make out the spire of the cathedral through a gap in the curtains.

Her captors had not noticed that Mash had already escaped. She'd gnawed away at a corner of the box, and even though she was also badly injured, she'd insisted on going for help.

Now Shandy was scared and all alone. She wished she was bigger and braver like Mash. She hoped the Twolegs would not be back for a very long time. She heard the cathedral bells chime ten and shivered in the cold, dark flat as the first snowflakes began to settle on the cars and empty streets below. It seemed like ages since she'd last seen her sister.

Shandy had no idea that Mash was now recovering from her wounds in the safety of the bridal shop in North Street. Big, tough Knuckles (the dog that everyone was a little scared of) had very gently carried Mash in his mouth all the way from the cross. Some of the other creatures had gasped as he'd loomed over her body with his mouth open wide, but his eyes were full of kindness as his jaws had ever so gently lifted the dazed hamster off the cold stone steps.

They'd managed to find a small corner at the back of the bridal shop that was full of discarded magazines and old samples of material and made Mash a sort of nest out of

satin and old lace. She'd slept for most of the next few days – sometimes kicking her legs wildly, as if trying to run. She would often call out her sister's name before drifting off to sleep again.

Knuckles and Streak visited the shop nearly every day to see how Mash was doing. Some of the birds brought her sunflower seeds from the bird tables scattered around town, and other creatures smuggled in fresh berries from the hedgerows. Caramella had been by her side ever since arriving with news about the strange letter.

'It's all so confusing,' whispered Mash weakly. 'If the letter was written by Gilbert's mum, then why is she not with him? It's just not like her. She would do anything to look after her son.'

'One has never understood Twolegs. We are constantly amazed that they ever manage to rear any children at all. One wonders how they have survive this long. We shall never understand them.'

'Well, I do know one thing,' replied Mash. 'I know where the mysterious clowns are, and it's time we paid them a visit!'

8 REINDEER LEAD THE WAY

It was Christmas Eve morning, and the owners of the bridal shop had shut early, as they decided that everyone was thinking more about Santa than weddings.

Mash had been nursed back to health by her new-found friends. She was now listening as Button briefed the gathered creatures on the plan. He'd spun an incredible web that resembled the centre of the city and was positioned at the centre where the cross would be. He had carefully created the streets leading from the cross in tiny strands of silk. Everything was to the correct scale so that it became a shimmering map that caught the early morning sun.

'So, do we all know what we are going to do?' he asked the rescue team. 'It's important that you're all in the right place at the right time, or else this is never going to work.'

'Can you go over the plan one more time?' spinked Codger. 'I'm not as young as I once was, and I tend to forget things. You know what they say, "A plan with a gap in it is like a hedge without a holly tree."'

They all glanced at each other, hoping that someone would be brave enough to ask what on earth the mole was talking about, but no one dared.

Button repeated the plan so that everybody knew where they had to be and what they had to do. An hour later, the bridal shop was left deserted. There was just a pile of ribbons and lace curled up in the corner, the remains of some hazel nuts and blackberries that the birds had collected, and a rather curious spider's web.

The first out of the shop was Blotch. His shiny red and black wing case became a blur as he flew off towards the cathedral. His job was to confirm that the freaky clowns and Shandy were in the house described by Mash. She'd said it was quite close to the library, just down a side street near the post office.

Mash had told everyone how she'd gnawed her way out of the cardboard box all those days ago and scampered to the front door. She'd waited patiently until the pizza-delivery boy arrived. The door had been open for just a few minutes, and she'd managed to squeeze through the open door just before it had slammed shut. A large wreath of plastic holly had crashed to the doorstep, missing her by just inches. It scattered fake berries and plastic reindeer on the doorstep as she'd limped across the street.

It had taken her ages to crawl the short distance to the Market Cross. At one point, she must have fainted. She'd awoken to see Roman gladiators towering over her and thought she must be having a bad dream. Then she'd realised it was the entrance to the Novium, the new museum built over the ruins of the Roman baths. Eventually she'd reached the cross and had been rescued by Knuckles.

Blotch was now counting the houses as he flew along by the Novium. He stopped for a moment to stare through the glass windows of the museum and thought how wonderful it must have been to bathe in the warm waters all those thousands of years ago when travelling so far from home. As the cold winter air swirled around him, he longed for his warm nest above the clothes driers in North Street. He shivered and flew on.

Just a few houses along, he

saw something glinting on the doorstep. It was a plastic reindeer covered in pink glitter. It lay there with a few strands of plastic holly. He knew he'd found the right place. Blotch landed on the sill of a top-floor window. Although the curtains were almost closed, he could make out cardboard boxes and half-eaten pizza. There were bunk beds in the corner and a small table and chair, but no sign of Gilbert or the missing hamster.

Blotch crawled through a small gap where the wooden window frame had rotted away. He flew over to the table and landed near a cold piece of Four Season's pizza. He held his breath and listened.

Outside, a small group of Twolegs were ringing the

doorbell of the house next door. They sang a few lines of "Silent Night", rang again, and added several lines from "Hark the Herald Angels Sing" before cursing slightly under their breath when the lights in the house went out.

It seemed that the Twolegs next door preferred to pretend they weren't home rather than listen to yet more Christmas carols screeched through their letterbox. The carol singers approached the door below, rang the bell, and started singing. The lights in this house also flicked off. When they reached "holy infant so tender and mild", they rang the bell again. This time the door opened.

Blotch heard someone tell the carol singers to go away, using words that had nothing to do with Christmas greetings and might have been the sort of thing a gladiator would say. He heard the door slam shut, and somebody stomped up the stairs and entered the room across the hall.

The ladybird nervously flew over to the door and landed just below it. Through the gap, he could see the feet of a couple of Twolegs who were watching telly. He silently crawled under the door into the room and flew as quietly as he could up to the naked light bulb hanging from the middle of the ceiling.

Below him, the Twolegs were drinking cans of beer and eating pizza. He could only see the top of their heads. One was clearly a male and the other a female. He needed to get a closer look to identify them. The lady Twoleg was complaining about the carol singers and how they had still rung the doorbell, even with the lights turned off. She stood up and switched the lights back on.

Blotch was suddenly blinded and fell from the light bulb, plummeting to the floor below. Dazed and confused, he lay on his back, wiggling his six legs in the air. His frantic attempts to get back on his feet caught the attention of the male Twoleg. He slurped the last dregs of beer from his can and smashed it firmly down on top of Blotch.

86

9 A CORONATION OF BEES

The smell of hotdogs and roasted chestnuts drifted from the stalls by the Market Cross. Knuckles was thinking of his next juicy steak. He always got lots of treats at Christmas, but that was still hours away. He cleared all thoughts of steaks and doggy snacks from his brain.

'Why has Blotch not confirmed the address by now?' asked Stitchley, who was nervously tucked under Knuckles' collar.

'I don't know,' replied Button,

as he tried to wriggle out from under the collar to get a better view.

The spiders were starting to itch a little, and Knuckles was trying hard not to scratch at his neck. He managed to keep control and just let out the tiniest of growls to hint to the spiders that they might want to keep still. They understood the message and stopped wriggling immediately.

After waiting for nearly an hour, it was agreed that Streak would go and look for the missing ladybird. He dashed along by the post office with his long, floppy ears tucked in as close as he could to keep him warm. He pretended that he was wearing a big woolly hat and imagined bouncing around on the beach to convince himself that he was not actually freezing to death.

None of the shoppers seemed to care that there was a puppy shivering in the cold. They were far too busy barging along the street, as if they were in a competition to buy as much as they could carry before midnight. Streak kept close to the big department store windows and tried to avoid the crowds. His fur was all fluffed up so he looked even cuter than normal. He turned the corner and headed up the street towards the museum. There was still no sign of Blotch. Where could he be?

He pushed on along the street and came across a group of carol singers who were counting their meagre earnings for the night. They were complaining about the weirdoes that had just moved in to the house further up the street. One of the carol singers said that his brother delivered pizza to them and he never ever got a tip.

'My brother says that they've only been there a few weeks and the house already stinks of curry and pizza. They have hardly any furniture, and the room is piled high with cardboard boxes. It's like they're on the run or something.'

Streak knew that he must be close. He saw two dustbins overflowing with rubbish just across the road. He raced over to them and sniffed at the bins. It was definitely Four Season's pizza and a little bit of leftover curried chicken. His mind wandered for a few minutes. He licked his lips at the thought of juicy chicken. Then there was a blast of warm air as the front door was opened wide. Streak crouched down low, hidden by the bins. He listened as a Twoleg pushed more rubbish into the overflowing bin. He dared to take a quick peek and saw Gilbert's mum disappear back into the house.

Streak raced back to tell the others that he'd found the house, but there was still no sign of Blotch. He'd seen Gilbert's mum, and she didn't look like she was being kept a prisoner. She looked tired and a bit angry.

'I don't get it,' said Stitchley. 'If she's okay, why haven't they gone to the police and said that they're safe? And where is Gilbert?'

'Perhaps they're just staying with her ex-husband and his new girlfriend until they find somewhere to live,' replied Button. 'Don't forget, their home burned down in the fire.'

They all agreed it was very confusing, but they would continue with the plan to rescue Shandy. If Caramella had done her work properly, help should be arriving soon.

Caramella had been one of the first to leave the bridal shop. She'd flown off in the direction of the Bishop's Palace Gardens, just behind the cathedral. She knew that she was not going to be the most popular queen bee, but this was an emergency. She'd spent the whole morning gently waking up her relations. Some of them weren't at all happy by this intrusion. Others took several nudges and kicks to waken from their hibernation. But by lunchtime, she'd gathered together a whole 'coronation' of queen bees.

She wasn't quite sure what the correct name was for a group of queens, but she decided that a 'coronation' sounded perfectly respectable. She addressed her royal cousins.

'We are gathered here today to support one's fellow creatures,' she began. 'It seems that some of the lowly creatures of our great and glorious city have been abducted. One cannot sit by and let this happen. We all have to make a stand! We shall fight them on the beaches; we shall fight them on the streets until we are victorious once again!'

Some of the other queen bees were shaking their heads from side to side. This was Caramella at her most royal, and one or two of them just wished she'd shut up and go back to sleep.

'We must swarm over to these cowards and strike them at their very hearts,' she continued. 'We shall never surrender. We shall fight to the death! Who is with me?'

'Can we go back to sleep then?' asked Queen Rosemary Minton-Parsley III, who lived in the flower shop opposite the cathedral. 'And do calm down, dear, you'll do yourself an injury. How long is this whole fiasco going to take? One has to get one's beauty sleep before the spring, you know. We older queens need more rest than you bright young things. We are not amused at being so rudely woken from our slumber!'

As most of the queen bees just wanted to get back to sleep, they all – somewhat reluctantly – agreed to follow Caramella in the direction of the Market Cross. The noise of the busy shoppers still haggling for last-minute bargains drowned out the buzz of twenty large black and yellow bumblebees settling around the turrets of the Market Cross.

Caramella flew down to the other creatures and very gently landed on Knuckles' nose. He almost went cross-eyed as the spiders updated Caramella with the latest news. It was now time for phase two of the plan – the

attack of the "killer bees!" Well, in truth, the attack of the slightly drowsy, I'd rather be home in bed, I wish Caramella would stop acting like queen of the universe – bees.

They flew off in a diamond formation in the direction of the museum.

10 THE HAMSTER ROPE TRICK

'I suppose it's time to feed her again,' said the man watching the telly.

'It's your turn. I fed her last time,' came the reply from his partner.

'I told you it was a bad idea keeping her here. She's been nothing but trouble ever since she arrived. And those carol singers nearly saw her.'

'Well, we couldn't exactly flush her down the loo, could we? She's a bit too big for that.'

The woman reluctantly pushed

her pizza aside, grabbed a clown mask from the shelf, and headed into the back room. The curtains were drawn tight, and the radiator had been turned off. The room was freezing. Among the cardboard boxes were a few blankets thrown on the floor, and lying there, tied to the radiator, was Gilbert's mum.

She stared at the masked figure as she approached her. She was sure she recognised the way she walked. The grimacing clown did not speak. She just thrust a bowl of food across the floor, turned on her heels, and was gone. Gilbert's mum closed her eyes and tried to remember where she'd seen this person before. From the corner of the room came a low squeaking noise. Gilbert's mum opened her eyes and looked over to the pile of boxes.

'It's okay, Shandy, we'll be all right,' she said to the pet hamster. 'They must be looking for us. I'm sure we'll be free before we know it.'

Shandy didn't reply. She was hungry and missed her sister. It had been days since Mash had escaped from the box, and Shandy had heard nothing yet. She longed to tell Gilbert's mum that help was on its way, but knew that she couldn't spink to her. Instead, she just made encouraging squeaking noises so that the brave Twoleg knew she wasn't alone.

Unfortunately, the message wasn't understood, and Gilbert's mum began to cry. She so missed her little boy and hoped he wasn't badly hurt. Her captors had made her write a letter to him saying everything would be fine. They told her that his dad was with him, and as long as she did exactly as they said, nobody would get hurt.

She reached out her hand to Gilbert's stepdad lying beside her. He'd tried to escape several times, and each time they'd pushed him back into the room. They must have put something in his food to make him sleepy, as he had been asleep now for almost twelve hours. She pushed her bowl of food away just in case it had also been drugged.

On the night of the fire, she remembered waking up in bed to see a strange masked figure in her room. Before she could let out a scream, another person had grabbed her and put a handkerchief with some horrible smelling chemical on it over her mouth. It'd made her drowsy, and she'd passed out. They'd done the same to her husband, and she could vaguely remember the voices arguing whether to leave them in the fire or to drag them out.

The rest of her memory was a vague mix of smoke, breaking glass, flashing blue lights, and sirens of the emergency services. For some reason she remembered clowns laughing and juggling balls of fire. She thought she'd seen giant hamsters blowing out the flames and spiders wrapping up her baby in strands of silk before carrying him away. Then she'd blacked out completely.

She'd awoken the next day with a banging headache and had been in this room ever since. Her captors assured her that Gilbert was alive. They even brought the newspaper to show her. It reported that he was recovering in hospital with his father by his side. She longed to see him and started to cry once more.

Shandy heard the sobbing and decided that she could wait no longer. Although she had promised her sister that she would keep watch over Gilbert's mum, she slid out through the hole in the box. She jumped down onto the floor and crawled over to the sobbing Twoleg. She squeaked a few times and pulled at her shoelace. Eventually, Gilbert's mum stopped crying and looked down at the little hamster.

'Oh, you poor thing. You're missing Gilbert too, aren't you? Don't worry, I'm sure he'll be here soon.'

Shandy gave the sole of her shoe a friendly little nibble. Then the hamster scampered out of the room in search of help. She squeezed under the gap below the door and found herself in a long corridor with several doors leading from it and stairs that obviously led down to the street. She could hear someone on the TV wishing everyone a happy Christmas and could smell food. *That must be the lounge,* she thought. She was about to head down the stairs when she heard muffled cries from the room to her left.

Shandy slowly slid under the

door and then stopped dead in her tracks. She couldn't believe her eyes. There was Gilbert tied to a chair with a piece of sticky tape across his mouth. He must have been here all along. She squeaked as loudly as she could and saw him turn towards her. Huge tears ran down his face as he saw his pet hamster in the doorway.

Shandy ran over to him and scrambled up his leg. Sitting on his knee, she squeaked again with tears in her own eyes. Gilbert struggled to reach her as his hands were tied tightly behind his back. Shandy felt helpless and wished that her bigger, stronger sister was here. Then Gilbert leaned forward in his chair. The hamster understood what he wanted her to do. She squeezed behind him and started gnawing at the rope that bound his hands.

She chewed and chewed at the rope until eventually it began to loosen. With one huge tug, Gilbert freed his hands and ripped off the tape from over his mouth. He scooped up his beloved hamster and smothered her with kisses. He held her to his cheek, still wet from his tears, and told her that she was the bravest, most beautiful hamster in the world.

Then there was a noise from the corridor. They heard footsteps approaching and the sound of keys being rattled, as if someone was searching for the right one to unlock his door. There was muttering and cursing and then the noise of a key sliding into the lock.

The door swung open, and

Gilbert's mum walked slowly over to the chair.

11 DOUBLE TROUBLE

Shandy's eyes almost popped out of her head. She couldn't work out how Gilbert's mum had managed to free herself from the radiator in the other room. Maybe she'd been pretending to be locked up all along. Were her tears all just a big act? It didn't make sense.

Then Gilbert said in a quiet trembling voice, 'You're not my mum. What have you done with her?'

Shandy stared unblinking at

the Twoleg once again. She was sure it was Gilbert's mum. She had the same hair and the same face, but her eyes were all wrong. They were cold and unfriendly. Shandy tried to make a run for the door but was quickly grabbed by the Twoleg, who lifted the hamster close to her face.

'You're a vile little rat, aren't you?' she spat out. 'We should have left you in those flames to fry.'

Shandy instantly realised that this was not the caring and loving Twoleg she'd known before. It must be her identical twin. It all made sense now. The Twoleg that Blotch had seen in the drycleaner's wasn't Gilbert's mum after all.

This was why they'd worn those scary clown masks all

along. Gilbert's dad suddenly appeared in the doorway. His face was drained of all colour. He simply could not believe that Gilbert had been tied to the chair. He would never have allowed that.

'What on earth do you think you're doing?' he demanded of the evil twin. 'Don't you ever touch my son again! Do you hear me? Ever!' He turned to Gilbert with tears in his eyes.

'Look, son, none of this was supposed to happen. We only wanted to cause a little damage to the pub so that your mother would sell it to us. She's always had everything. She has you and a lovely home. It just isn't fair!'

Gilbert couldn't believe his ears.

'You've got to believe me,

son. I never meant it to go this far. It was just supposed to scare your mum a bit. We never meant to hurt anyone. I'm so sorry. You were the first one I came for. I would never let anything bad happen to you.'

'So who is she?' asked Gilbert, regarding the twin warily. 'And where's the young girlfriend you were with at the hospital?'

'It was me, you fool,' said the evil twin. 'I thought you'd seen through my fake lips and ridiculous blonde wig when we came to visit. You really are a dumb kid, aren't you?'

She was still holding on to Shandy as she glared at Gilbert, but had loosened her grip just a little. Shandy bit down hard on her thumb. The evil twin shrieked and dropped the hamster to the floor. Shandy gasped in pain as her tiny paws were still tender from the fire. She ran out of the door into the hallway.

'Leave the hamster,' said Gilbert's dad weakly. His body seemed to sag with exhaustion. 'This has gone far enough. We need to stop now.'

Shandy's heart was beating so fast that she thought it might burst. She squeezed back under the door of the room where Gilbert's real mum was still tied to the radiator. Looking up at the window, she saw a swarm of queen bees hovering just outside. Shandy struggled up the leg of a nearby chair, then with all her strength, leapt onto the window ledge. She jumped up and down, hoping Caramella would see her.

Caramella did, indeed, see Shandy bouncing up and down like a jack-in-the-box, and knew this was the right flat. She turned to her coronation of bees and shouted, 'To the front door, ladies. This will be our finest hour!'

The buzzing grew louder as all twenty queen bees dove in formation towards the door at street level. The letterbox was partially stuffed with fliers and leaflets promoting last-minute gifts. They flew through the gap and swarmed up the stairs.

They could hear yelling coming from one of the rooms at the top of the stairs and flew with great haste towards the noise. The Twolegs were shouting furiously at each other. The male Twoleg said that the female one was a mad witch.

He wished he'd never met her. She grabbed Gilbert roughly by the collar and said that she hadn't gone to all this bother for nothing. She wasn't leaving empty handed.

That was good enough for Caramella. She screamed, 'Charge!' and the bees headed towards the evil twin, who waved her arms around her head and screamed as they attacked her. She picked up a tea towel that had been lying on the floor and waved it around madly like a flag of surrender. But still the bees attacked. She stumbled into the hallway with a dozen or so buzzing around her head, and went tumbling wildly down the stairs.

Still screaming and waving the towel around her head, she

rushed out into the street and bowled into a group of carol singers who were halfway through "God Rest Ye Merry Gentleman". The startled singers stood open-mouthed as the screaming woman disappeared around the corner into West Street.

They hardly noticed as two dogs bounded up the stairs to the flat above. Seeing his son tied up was clearly just too much for Gilbert's dad to bear. He slumped in the corner of the room with his head in his hands, crying like a baby. Gilbert reached out to comfort his dad.

All this time Streak had been sniffing up and down the corridor. He gently nudged Gilbert's hand and then led him to the room opposite. Knuckles stood guard over his father as Gilbert opened the door. As his eyes adjusted to the dark, he saw his mum and stepdad straining at the ropes that bound them. The evil twin must have also placed tape over their mouths as they had both nearly turned blue as they tried to shout for help.

Gilbert flew through the door and ripped the tape off first his mum's face and then his stepdad's. It seemed to take forever to untie the ropes. They grasped each other in a three-way hug, and tears soaked their faces. His mum promised to never let him out of her sight again. His stepdad ruffled his hair and kissed his neck, hardly able to speak at all.

Shandy lay exhausted on the windowsill. She was relieved that she had managed to attract Caramella's attention. She just wanted to sleep now. She closed her eyes and heard, 'Are you going to lie up there all day, or are you going to come and give your sister a hug?'

Shandy looked down at the floor and saw her twin sister clinging for dear life to Streak's collar. Mash had nearly slipped off twice as they'd dashed up the stairs. Streak gently lowered his head and allowed the injured hamster to step onto the floor.

Shandy jumped down from the window ledge, and the sisters nuzzled each other and squeaked in delight, knowing that they were all safe. The plan had been a great success, and they couldn't wait to go and tell Button and Stitchley, who had remained back at the Market Cross.

'Has anyone see Blotch?' asked Mash. 'He was supposed to come on ahead to make sure we were at the right place.'

Nobody replied.

12 DIGGING FOR VICTORY

The hugging and sobbing was interrupted by Knuckles barking from the other room. Gilbert's mum followed Streak across the hall. She gasped when she saw her ex-husband cowering on the floor like a frightened kitten. He was still shaking his head and mumbling that he was sorry. Gilbert's stepdad had a look of thunder on his face. He stepped towards the broken man on the floor, but Gilbert's mum put her arm out to stop him.

She knelt down by the

sobbing man and very gently held his hand. Both dogs quietly left the room so that the Twolegs gathered there could be alone. It was going to be a very difficult time for everyone.

'It's the season of goodwill and forgiveness,' spinked Shandy. 'I'll never understand Twolegs. They can be so cruel and mean, even to the ones they love.'

'Well, I think that Twoleg has a lot of explaining to do,' spinked Knuckles, 'and some of it might be down at the police station. But let's look for Blotch, he must be here somewhere.'

The creatures searched the hall and found nothing, so they entered the lounge. The TV was still blaring out Christmas messages for anyone who had failed to notice that it was now just hours away. It was showing people in Australia floating in the sea on blow-up reindeer, wearing Santa hats, and waving at the camera in the blazing sun.

Streak sniffed the air for any sign of Blotch. He picked up a rather dreadful smell coming from a corner of the room. Knuckles had smelled it too. They led the hamsters over to a table. Stale pieces of pizza were curling at the edges, and there was a half-finished beer can on the floor. They sniffed at the beer can and feared the worst. Streak gently pushed it over with his nose.

The horrible smell filled the room. All they could see were traces of yellow blood. Streak very nervously examined the bottom of the beer can. Shandy couldn't look and turned her face away. There, curled up in a tight ball, was Blotch – shaken but still alive.

'We saw the blood and thought you were dead,' spinked Shandy, 'and what's that awful smell?'

'A little ladybird trick,' replied Blotch. 'We can release blood from our knees when under attack, and I'm afraid it's a bit pongy! I'm sorry, but it was rather an emergency.'

'Now I've heard everything,' spinked Knuckles. 'What's next? Spiders firing darts from their eyes? Talking of which, we need to get back to the cross and let Button and Stitchley know the good news. Oh, and Blotch, don't ever do that stinky-blood-from-the-knees thing near me again!'

As they crept past the Twolegs, they saw that Gilbert was hand-in-hand with his mum. His stepfather was just putting away his mobile phone, and the sirens of a police car could be heard in the distance. The little band of creatures headed back to the cross, with Blotch and the hamsters all hitching a ride on Streak's back.

Over at the cross, the spiders had been waiting patiently throughout the night for news, when they saw a Twoleg come screaming down West Street. She was waving a white tea towel in the air like a mad woman. They peered out from the arches of the Market Cross as she dashed towards her car parked opposite the post office.

Still shouting and flapping her arms, she jumped into her car and emptied the entire contents of her handbag on the seat until she found her lipstick..

A smug smile crossed her face as she realised she'd escaped the coronation of angry bees. Caramella and the other queen bees buzzed angrily around the car. The Twoleg winced in pain at some of the bee stings but was composed enough to open her lipstick and apply a large red smear of it over her lips. *I'm finally going to escape this boring town and my hopeless boyfriend*, she thought. *My twin sister can have him back for all I care. He's weak and useless. I'm better off without him.*

She started the engine, flipped on the headlights, and

put the car in reverse, intending to turn around and head for the coast, but it came to a shuddering halt. She twisted in her seat to see what was wrong. She had reversed into the largest mole hill that she'd ever seen. Soil clogged up the exhaust pipe, and fumes began to fill the car.

Panic was now written all over her face. She crunched the car into first gear, and it shot forward, but not for long. The front tyres suddenly disappeared through the tarmac into a deep hole. They spun furiously as soil was sprayed into the air. Codger had done his work well. He'd gathered some of the younger moles together earlier that day, and they'd spent hours and hours digging and tunnelling around the car. All that waiting and watching had paid off. Several of the creatures had observed suspicious looking Twolegs sneaking into their car late at night and they'd made sure that Button and Stitchley had been kept up to date.

Codger peered out into the gloom as a police car screeched to a halt. The sound of buzzing faded to a low hum. The bells of the cathedral chimed twelve. It was Christmas day.

It was not exactly a jolly time for Gilbert and his mum. The evil twin was locked away and doctors said that she was quite mad. She would rock back and forth in her bed buzzing like a bee. Gilbert's dad had been released and was receiving help from specialist doctors at the hospital. The kidnapping and escape from the fire made news all over again. The local paper splashed pictures of the almost identical twins on the front page. The evil twin had confessed to being jealous of her sister all her life and admitted to having tricked Gilbert's dad into going along with her wicked plan. After a few days, the reporters and photographers drifted away and finally left Gilbert and his family alone.

They'd been given rooms in a hotel, but it was not like home. He longed for the day when he could return to his own room. At least he had his hamsters with him. Gilbert's mum had bought them the biggest, shiniest cage he'd ever seen. It had slides and wheels and tunnels to crawl through. Shandy and Mash loved it. They had no way of telling her that there were so many other creatures to thank. But they knew they couldn't have done it alone.

Blotch returned to his family, who were still fast asleep above the warm air vents in the dry cleaner's. Codger would tell the story of the time he captured the evil twin for many years to come. He even sometimes remembered to mention one or two of the other creatures. Caramella was already fast asleep, dreaming of warm summer evenings. The dogs were spoiled rotten with goodies and Christmas treats, and Button and Stitchley returned to their quiet, peaceful bridal shop for a well-deserved rest.

This was going to be one Christmas that they would all never forget.

Special thanks to Azra and the twins for
the inspiration for this book

ABOUT THE AUTHOR

Christopher Joyce is a Twoleg from Chichester in West Sussex, England. He has been a teacher, marketing director, waiter, once made Venetian blinds, worked in a steel works and has run a garden design business.

Also by Christopher Joyce

The Creatures of Chichester:
the one about the stolen dog

The Creatures of Chichester:
the one about the curious cloud

Find out more at
www.creaturesofchichester.com

Made in the USA
Charleston, SC
12 October 2014